SOFIA MARTINEZ

Shopping ~Trip~ Trouble

by Jacqueline Jules

illustrated by Kim Smith

PICTURE WINDOW BOOKS
a capstone imprint

Sofia Martinez is published by
Picture Window Books, a Capstone imprint
1710 Roe Crest Drive
North Mankato, MN 56003
www.mycapstone.com

Library of Congress Cataloging-in-Publication data
is available on the Library of Congress website.

ISBN: 978-1-5158-0729-2 (library binding)
ISBN: 978-1-5158-0731-5 (paperback)
ISBN: 978-1-5158-0733-9 (eBook PDF)

Summary: It's time to go school shopping, and Sofia
is extra excited about her new supplies. But that
excitement turns to panic when her cousin Manuel
goes missing. With Sofia's entire family on the case,
Manuel won't be missing for long.

Designer: Aruna Rangarajan
Art Director: Kay Fraser

J
SERIES
SOFIA

Printed and bound in the USA.
010838S18

TABLE OF CONTENTS

Chapter 1
Backpack Decisions 5

Chapter 2
Missing Manuel 10

Chapter 3
Back to the Backpacks 17

CHAPTER 1

Backpack Decisions

Sofia hurried to keep up with her two older sisters, Elena and Luisa. Elena and Luisa hurried to keep up with Mamá, Tía Carmen, and Sofia's four cousins.

The whole family was going school shopping. They were a big group!

"Stay close," Tía Carmen said. "I don't want anyone to get lost."

They went to the backpack aisle first. The backpacks were hanging from the ceiling to the floor.

"Should I pick soccer or baseball?" Hector asked.

"Should I pick zebra stripes or flowers?" Elena asked.

"I pick dinosaurs!" Alonzo said.

"Look at this one!" Manuel yelled. He was pointing to a huge backpack with leopard spots.

"You're in preschool," Hector told his little brother. "That bag is too big for you."

"No it's not," Manuel said.

"It is a little big," Sofia said. "Maybe you should pick something else."

"Fine," Manuel said, yawning. He was too tired to argue.

Just then Sofia saw a bright green bag. It had a cool feather design.

"Peacock feathers!" she shouted. "¡Perfecto!"

"¡Vámonos!" Mamá said. "We have more things to buy."

CHAPTER 2

Missing Manuel

Sofia was excited to see all the pretty notebooks.

"Mamá," she said. "How many can I have?"

Mamá looked at the school supply list. "Tres."

Three notebooks! That meant she could have the rainbow, the silver, and the green!

Mamá read item after item from the list. Everyone was busy picking things out.

Sofia took a break and looked around. Something didn't seem right.

Sofia counted the kids. She came up with three cousins and two sisters. There should be seven kids, not six. She counted the kids again. Oh, no!

"Manuel!" Sofia shouted. "He's not here!"

"Where is my little Manuel?"
Tía Carmen cried.

Sofia's family ran around the store. They called Manuel's name.

They rushed around so fast that Hector bumped into Alonzo. Then Alonzo bumped into a shelf of crayons and paint bottles.

Crayons and bottles rolled everywhere! Sofia, Hector, and Alonzo tried to clean up, but it was a big mess.

A store employee came by. "Don't worry. I'll get someone to help," she said.

"Gracias," Sofia said.

Sofia's family kept looking for Manuel. They were very worried.

Then they heard a voice over the loudspeaker. That gave Sofia an idea.

"Could we ask the lady on the loudspeaker to help find Manuel?" she asked.

"¡Claro!" Tía Carmen said. "Follow me!"

CHAPTER 3

Back to the Backpacks

"Attention! A four-year-old boy is missing. He has black hair and is wearing a blue shirt. Please come to the front of the store if you've seen him."

After the announcement, an older man came up to them.

"I saw a little boy in the backpack aisle," he said. "He had black hair and a blue shirt."

"¡Gracias!" Mamá said. "¡Vámonos!"

When the family reached the backpack aisle, they only saw the huge wall of backpacks. No Manuel.

Baby Mariela began to cry. Tía Carmen brushed Mariela's cheek. "I know. It's your nap time," she said.

As Tía Carmen comforted the baby, Sofia thought of something.

"It's Manuel's nap time, too," she said.

That's when she saw a row of backpacks on the bottom move. Sofia pushed one aside. Manuel was underneath, fast asleep.

Tía Carmen grabbed Manuel.

"You scared me!"

Everyone gathered around
Manuel to hug him. He rubbed his
eyes. "I want to go home," he said.

When the family got back

home, they had lunch together.

Just as they finished, Sofia asked,

"What about our school supplies?"

Mamá slapped her forehead.

"We left everything in the shopping cart at the store!" she said.

"Can we go back?" Sofia asked.

"Mañana," Tía Carmen said. "I'm too tired now."

"Sí," Mamá agreed. "Tomorrow."

"What if the things we picked are gone?" Sofia asked.

"Por favor," Elena said. "My butterfly notebooks were so pretty."

"I want the shark pencil case," Hector said.

"And I really love that backpack with the feathers on it," Sofia said.

Everyone remembered how long it took to choose school supplies.

Mamá sighed and picked up her purse. "¡Vámonos!"

Sofia was the first one out the door.
Manuel was right behind her. He was
ready to go again!

Spanish Glossary

claro — of course

gracias — thank you

mamá — mom

mañana — tomorrow

perfecto — perfect

por favor — please

sí — yes

tía — aunt

tres — three

vámonos — let's go

Talk It Out

1. Do you think Manuel should have gotten in trouble for leaving the group? Why or why not?

2. Do you think Manuel was scared? Why or why not?

3. Did you know what was going to happen? Go back through the story and find at least two clues that would help you guess.

Write It Down

1. Pretend you are Sofia. Write a journal entry about your day.

2. Make a list of ten items you need for school. Then add one more item you wish you could get for school.

3. Write three sentences about shopping, each including a Spanish word that was used in the story.

About the Author

Jacqueline Jules is the award-winning author of thirty children's books, including *No English* (2012 Forward National Literature Award), *Zapato Power: Freddie Ramos Takes Off* (2010 Cybils Literary Award, Maryland Blue Crab Young Reader Honor Award, and ALSC Great Early Elementary Reads), and *Freddie Ramos Makes a Splash* (named on 2013 List of Best Children's Books of the Year by Bank Street College Committee).

When not reading, writing, or teaching, Jacqueline enjoys time with her family in northern Virginia.

About the Illustrator

Kim Smith has worked in magazines, advertising, animation, and children's gaming. She studied illustration at the Alberta College of Art and Design in Calgary, Alberta.

Kim is the illustrator of the middle-grade mystery series *The Ghost and Max Monroe*, the picture book *Over the River and Through the Woods*, and the cover of the middle-grade novel *How to Make a Million*. She resides in Calgary, Alberta.

FUN
doesn't stop here!

- Videos & Contests
- Games & Puzzles
- Friends & Favorites
- Authors & Illustrators

Discover more at
www.capstonekids.com

See you soon!
¡Nos Vemos pronto!